I Can Hear Me Fine

I Can Hear Me Fine

Jean Smith

Get to the Point ▶ Publishing
Vancouver, Canada

I Can Hear Me Fine

Get to the ▶ Point Publishing
304–1320 Salsbury Drive
Vancouver, B.C.
Canada V5L 4B3

Front cover photo by Marty Perez
Back cover photo by Jon Snyder
Typeset by Vancouver Desktop Publishing Centre Ltd.
Printed and bound in Canada

Distributed by Arsenal Pulp Press
100–1062 Homer Street
Vancouver, B.C.
Canada V6B 2W9

Canadian Cataloguing in Publication Data

Smith, Jean, 1959–
I can hear me fine

ISBN 0-9697112-0-4

I. Title.
PS8587.M58I2 1993 C813′.54 C93-091593-3
PR9199.3.S55I2 1993

CONTENTS

Once there was the soft glow of a flare sent, an amber fragment knocking out the sky. Then there was the darkness after too much light. At twelve o'clock, across the table, a black wall. At ten o'clock, a woman wearing a white fur coat isn't thinking about death in blood and teeth and snow.

Blocks of mustard coloured panels are beside the black and the needles on the ground that Joelle never sees. Joelle wants to be the green next to the black in the bass line. Her teeth are set hard against one another, she is looking out the window. It is autumn. It is still warm out, but the sun is coming down at an angle that is autumn. Animated death. It is not summer.

Joelle is eighteen. The grape leaves have gone yellow. She looks at them in relation to the blue sky.

She is washing a frying pan. Her boyfriend is in the living room watching TV. Joelle hates pancakes, but that's what was in the frying pan. The pan comes out of the soapy water. Joelle slams it into the arborite counter, right on the edge, more pressure per square inch. Steel and blue flash together with all the historic energy of the situation.

Pale moon of a half face waking, yellowed up by fear. Lie flat in the rusted cage, the lock is sealed with wax. The bone hinges are brittle and split. Every creaking motion releases the scent of blackened spice, crystals splinter and hiss against the sun.

A photograph tells you that the old woman is looking at the young woman with disapproval. X took the shot knowing you would think that. It is in a silver frame, the frame makes it even more convincing.

Accidentally Joelle built the name, accidentally Joelle built the night. Cheap jewelry flew across the dance floor, nuggets came unglued from his wrist, plastic gems pulled away from the claws on Joelle's rings.

Sunlight comes into the kitchen, grey. All the windows are covered in plastic. A dull warmth hits the floor, the table and the guy sitting at the table. He can't finish a sentence. He can barely get one started. The woman at the stove is not diluted, she thinks about things and tells people her ideas, but he can't finish a sentence.

"It's a piece of cake, so cut the crap," she says.

Her voice is like dirty water being squeezed out of cheap sponge. She tells people the little things, she tells people about his bad habits. She can't let it go with love, she has to make sure she can't go back. She runs out of the house with both guns smoking to face the cameras.

"Why did you do it Joelle?"

"He didn't wash enough and there was always mud on the kitchen floor."

Joelle and the violinist, the guy, go camping on an island. He can't build a fire. The sun is burning him. He has a raging headache. Joelle's hair is packed with smoke, her eyes are red. She scrapes oysters around in a frying pan muttering, "These things smell insane."

The violinist has had it, he is going home. Joelle has had it with him, but she doesn't believe he'll go. She sits by the smoking fire pit a long time. She closes her eyes when the smoke comes her way. The guy at the next campsite can build a fire. Night is coming. Joelle is alone except for the fire builder and the bunch of greasy guys with plaid shirts and motorcycles they end up drinking beer with. Joelle doesn't like any of the men as the sun goes down. She is afraid to be unaligned. She watches them develop in time and beer. More bikers arrive, their headlights cutting into campfire smoke and flames.

The violinist reappears in the city, his headaches and clean hands aren't as noticeable here, here in Joelle's attic apartment, six blocks from where his mother washes the cum out of his socks and makes him breakfast.

The violinist goes to the hospital. The headaches will not go away. He is committed to the psychiatric ward. Joelle visits him there, he is watching TV in the lounge, wearing pyjamas, smoking a foreign cigarette. The smoke is sweet. His legs are crossed, a leather slipper dangles off his foot. He seems to be enjoying himself.

"My psychiatrist says you're the cause of my problems Joelle. You are causing my headache. My mother is a contributing factor too. I'm happy to be here, away from both of you."

Joelle is nine. Every Sunday afternoon she watches a TV show about sex. Her mother watches it with her. A balding doctor in a white coat sits on the edge of a desk. He talks about sperm, ovaries and fallopian tubes.

Joelle is eleven. The TV series is over. Her mother is standing beside a blackboard in the laundry room. She has printed the names of the male and female reproductive organs on the board. Drawing on the blackboard is a lot less fun, even after the words womb and penis have been erased.

Joelle is thirteen. A boy she likes is walking behind her on the sawdust path beside the playing field. Joelle thinks the sawdust looks fake spread out on the ground, making a path through the woods. The woods look fake too, the trees are small and awkward. The branches are thin, making the forest transparent.

The boy comes up behind Joelle, he pushes her. She is on the ground, she is trying to get away, but the boy is sitting on her stomach. Quickly, as if he'd done it a hundred times before, he reaches under her shirt and grabs her breast. He twists it, hard, demanding a name, an answer.

Joelle is walking home with sawdust in her undershirt. She is trying to walk as if nothing is wrong. Her undershirt is all twisted and pulled, but she can't straighten it out until she gets home. The red tulips are so strong against the green lawns.

Joelle is walking through the narrow streets of the market. People are too busy to stare at her. She looks out of place, she feels out of place. Her long blond hair is tied back with a piece of ribbon she bought in the market. She knows she paid too much for the blood red ribbon, but it was still cheap.

Joelle is walking into the flower market. Old men are stringing blossoms into long chains, they will be sold and left in the temple. Joelle thinks about flowers, she tries to keep her own ideas about flowers quiet. She wonders if people are obligated to buy them, if there are different flowers for different prayers. She would like to ask her lover about the flowers, there are a few other things she would like to ask him, but he doesn't speak English and she doesn't speak whatever it is that he speaks.

Joelle goes to the small store where vials of flower oils are sold. Gardenia, hibiscus. She has been buying the tiny bottles, wrapping them in newspaper and mailing them to her mother. There are no letters, just the crudely made glass vials with pieces of cork shoved in them. The thick perfumes are dirty greens and yellows. Joelle's mother has eighteen bottles of the putrid oils standing on the shelf behind her bathroom mirror. She opens the cabinet and sees them all lined up in there.

"Damn, where is that girl?"

She slams the mirrored door and a glitter of little bottles falls on the glass shelf.

The man Joelle lives with is the cook in the hotel. She had been very sick, he had taken care of her, bringing her glasses of water and bananas. He was gentle and concerned. He wanted to touch her long blond hair.

The cook lives on the roof of the hotel. He climbs up there on a ladder made of branches tied together. Joelle has been climbing up there too. It's a beautiful place to wake up. The sky gets pink and then the bells start. The old guy on the roof next door has three goats. He brings straw up for them and makes his tea over a little fire.

Joelle keeps her room in the hotel. No one has seen her climbing up the ladder to the roof. She is not sure what people would think about it. She doesn't like this feeling, she wants to know what she is doing, but every night she climbs the ladder and curls into the warm arms of the man who holds her, looks at her and touches her with strong love.

Joelle has forgotten some of their names, she has forgotten some of them altogether. One of them was quite sincere. He twirled Joelle around in his arms and sighed. Dancing, his eyes never left her. He smiled, laughed and moved with her. He tried to set up situations where things might progress between them. His eyes worked hard on her. She watched them. He started to tell other men not to talk to her. He didn't tell them not to talk this way or that way, he told them not to talk to her at all.

Joelle's eyes focused on the jungle beyond them. In slow motion she turned her head to face him. Two thousand years later her eyes met his. She finished the breath that she had started in the jungle. In slow motion she exhaled a cloud of steam.

"Fuck off," she said.

"Didn't that night mean anything to you Joelle?"

"No."

"You could have told me that before I wasted all this time."

Two thousand years.

Joelle is listening to a phone-in radio show. The host of the show says the switchboard is jammed.

"I'm thirty-five, my name is Helen, actually that's my middle name. I want a guy who's sensitive, honest, likes the outdoors, movies, going for walks. I was married once, ten years ago. I haven't met anyone, you know, really met anyone since. I guess I just want a guy to call my own. Maybe we'll have kids one day."

"OK, that was Helen, " says the host. "She wants a guy who likes the outdoors, she's a lonely gal who hasn't met anyone for ten years. OK, here's our next caller. Hi, go ahead."

Joelle is twenty and the ball is coming right at her. The guy from third base is running towards her yelling, "I'll get it, I'll get it."

The example is walking towards Joelle. He is talking about health. Complaints. He is talking about his wife. Divorce. He is talking about money. Taxes. He is talking about his plans. Grandiose.

Joelle is dancing with the example, she stops to listen to how much his legs hurt. He is spitting in her eyes. He should be quiet for ten years.

It is dark out. Joelle walks across the parking lot and meows at a small white bag of garbage. She opens the door to her apartment. From the living room she hears, “I feel like balling.”

He has been sitting on her couch for two days wrapped in a yellow sheet. He has great hair.

“Bowling?” Joelle asks as she puts down her bag of groceries on the kitchen counter.

He is gone. Joelle goes into the bathroom. Her whizzing pee sounds exactly like the Flight of the Bumblebee. She pulls up her pants, leans across the sink towards the mirror and spreads lip gloss over her mouth, turning her lips into slices of roast beef. They shimmer that same blue-green as the roast beef at a deli, like oil on wet pavement.

Joelle goes into the bedroom to find dry socks. One foot is wet. She tried on a cowboy boot at Value Village. It was soaking wet inside. Joelle goes back to the bathroom, draws black lines around her eyes and puts on her brown leather jacket.

Downtown, in a club, faces as smooth and dry as sand dunes float past her. Joelle listens, she wants to know what people are talking about. They are motioning above their heads; bursting, twisting, smoothing motions. They are talking about hairdos.

Slow purple fish break the surface. Heavy blossoms have dropped down from the trees. The flower segments float. Black lake. The sky is a whirlpool of yellow. Claudine smells the smoke of an ancient fire burning in the back of the woods. A small group of men are sitting there talking, she doesn't want to hear what they're saying. She runs through the stream of a new sensation, running from the back of the woods. The smile on her face is as bright as the fish scales, she doesn't want to be in the woods.

It is raining. The sky is swirling tighter. Claudine is wet, her white shirt is stuck to her, she pulls at it. The fabric is transparent, the shirt looks pink. Her black velvet pants are heavy, they have stretched down with the weight of water. Claudine trips over them. She takes them off and leaves them in a pile.

The black velvet absorbs light and heat. The sky is darkening down to purple.

Claudine opens an iron gate. It scrapes across the path, chipping up bits of loose cement. The noise scares wet birds into the sky.

They fly up, taken by the circling motion. They are gone.

Claudine walks barefoot across the muddy, rutted yard, through puddles, towards a barn and the sound of horses shifting their weight in the darkness. As she gets closer she sees clouds of steam pushing out from the stall doors. She steps up onto the bottom rail of the fence and swings her leg up, her bare thigh brushes against a wet horse. She sits on the fence waiting for her eyes to adjust, breathing in the smell of straw and horses. She jumps down into the muddy stall, a horse snaps its head up and its solid face hits Claudine under her chin. She pounds her fist into its rump and moves farther into the darkness until she feels dry straw under her feet. The straw is heaped up, warm. Claudine falls into it, sweeping it over herself with both arms.

Marcus takes part of her face, tangerine face, and makes it the side of a cliff. Just to test it, just to see.

He takes her in his taxi to see the sun. The tires squeal, the two way radio feeds back. He drives fast, trying to find a place to see the sun before it's too late. Claudine is wearing overalls, she is holding needle nose pliers and baling wire.

"Sometimes the oranges roll out into the street," Marcus says.

The orange juice factory is shooting mashed orange peels into a baby blue dumpster. The smell is heavy.

"If you ask for a couple they'll usually give them to you."

Marcus takes Claudine to his favourite intersection. It is dark. He ducks his head, looking out the windows, driving slow. He tries to explain why it's his favourite intersection. Railway tracks cross it at an angle. The street turns to dirt on the other side.

"The train track lights flash red," he says. " The colour stays in your brain, glowing there, after the lights are out."

Claudine talks about light, yellow light, she says it glows more than other light. They are looking at the light surrounding the coloured bulbs on the patio of an Italian restaurant. After dinner Marcus says,

"The falling stars here leave green tails."

They both look into the dark sky.

"How do they know where the stars are? Light comes all that way, bending in the gravitational pull of every planet it passes," Claudine says.

Marcus gives Claudine his business card from Yellow Cab. He has filled in his name as Super Man Side In.

The thoughts that become words flow simply. The things that surround those thoughts fall away, grey to him. Indistinct. They turn to emotion, a contrast to the words.

The fish are purple in the tank. They swim, smooth muscled, through the murky water. Coming towards the glass their colour intensifies. Claudine feels them hidden, passing against the weeds. Lightning reverses everything to a shattering bright blue. X-ray. The violence of electricity takes control, demanding entry.

The train pounds through, echoing off the corrugated metal shed in the back. Claudine can't sleep through the dense roar. She watches the light on the ceiling, she makes it swirl in ellipses, it leaves imprints on her eyes.

Claudine tries to go beyond the room, she tries to break the connection between her and Marcus. She feels the energy shifting, she follows it out the window into her own thoughts. The train helps.

Pulling. She is almost there now, he must sense it, he calls her back. He reveals himself, almost as if there was no risk.

Watching themselves they alter what they are. Selecting, focusing, taking a colour and naming it, altering it. Lavender, purple, mauve. Adding contrast by saying, "Yellow."

Arc of moon coming up. Learning to think with words. Afraid that she can't make anything real with words.

Marcus is on the other side of the fence, fenced in with the dog, saying, "Pretty big dog."

Dishes in the sink, cutlery rusting. Egg shells in the dirt. A lighter just sparks. It slides across the floor heading for the garbage. Faces sad. Falling. To the ground. Leaving what was never there to begin with.

Rain. Vanishing before it hits the ground. Back up. Leaving what was never there.

Hot streets. Unripe fruit. Sliced. Salted. Rind on the ground.

A memory of juice. Another time. Another hot day. Wanting to make from nothing. Ripeness. Sweetness.

This river flows bright green. Fast on the surface. Below. Waiting in cool. Stillness.

Resisting the falling patterns. There never was empty. There never was full. Whole. No starting time. Place where it was warm.

Hands make shapes. Smooth big hands. Softness. Hardness. Hands making the word box. Thinking that hand is so hard that it is, for a second, a box.

Impossible to be pure. Walking, falling, sad, back to the ground. His hands are making the words box, sick, listen, take.

Living in the white spaces, searching them out of everything.

Settling into night. Smear of sun hitting the crossing clouds. A clear space that will last, made from the thread of agreement, pulled from aggression. Once only, a falsely lasting life. The blaze that softens to stillness, the heat that paralyses everything but now. Wash of plainness found in a slow blurred state. Day again, night. Holding down time, testing light and tension against emptiness. Amber dripping off its own edges, her edges melting in whole rays. Rain filling the streets with warm water. Keeping this measurement, Claudine invents the end. When she moves in quick, deliberate turns, then it will end, threatened. She is a threat.

This is a stopping place. She has time.

So it starts here, in a clearness, so clear because of what surrounds it.

This river is a powder green line, fast on the surface. Marked water. Soft underneath.

Just like that, there was a beginning.

Land without value. Imprint. Walking into the

sky, hill rolling back, accommodating the twist of the desert. Slow steps. Flattened season. Thick beneath feet, under sky, looking up.

Smoke blowing into the house. The fences between the yards are down. Isolated language. Eyes aching, waiting to see, flickering nervously.

A model enclosed in a plexiglass case; the canyon, the cactus and the orange pools. Glued down sand for rocks, cut cardboard mountains. Bending over to look down. Absorbing size. Waiting without intention. Pressed down by the sky, concealed strength. Below. Bending, falling into what used to be big.

Claudine made the model. The picture explodes, falling back to recognized systems. Hill after hill folding back into themselves. Repeating patterns. Patterns of weight. Mouths thick with songs never sung, open, full. Calling water's freedom, pushing up over a shallow spot.

Leaning out of the passenger seat to keep seeing the moon, the mountain, the light on the desert behind. Ripple texture. Riverbeds are dry, pavement turns to sand, going to the other side of the mountain.

Claudine always wants to call grey what is black, but here the pigs must be fed. Jars. Half full. Raspberries.

Claudine holds the palm of her hand flat against the pig's nose.

She didn't know pigs ate egg shells. Triangles of shell on wet noses. Dividing up the universe, she is never satisfied. Begging. Silent. Two shadows. Leaf shadow on the surface. Sunk below in cool, shadow's shadow is softer on its edges. Water holds light. Fluid. Moving.

Claudine wants a sound for the shadows. Commonly recognizable, the black shapes on the walls are other rooms.

Claudine used to have smooth black hair. She still does, but it doesn't matter any more. A man might think she's singing while she braids her hair, she is not, she braids her hair while she sings.

"Marcus, can you give me some advice?"

Claudine is in Marcus's lap in the swivel armchair. She is wearing cut off jeans and a white t-shirt. Her head is resting on Marcus's chest, her bare legs hang over the arm of the chair. The room is quiet except for the squeak of the chair rocking back and forth. After a while Marcus asks, "About what?"

"Oh, I mean general advice," Claudine says and starts to sit up. Marcus tightens his hold around her waist and Claudine falls back against him.

"Well, I think you should ease up on yourself. Quit looking for patterns in everything. You always have to be doing something."

There are tests in the desert. Everything is fine, people always pant like dogs. Grouped together in armchairs, they are developing strategies. The friends of the people who invent board games think they should get a cut when it finally goes into mass production. Some of the ideas were theirs after all, even if they were just joking. Distance, horse speed and gunshot equation.

The trains shake the house when they go by. The whistle blows about a quarter of a mile down and then the light shines slowly across the walls, changing speed on different angles in the room. The ratio of noise and light is always the same on north bound trains, they are the ones leaving town, picking up speed. Claudine is used to the noise now, but tonight they are both awake listening to a train go by so slowly. Marcus takes half a cigarette out of the ashtray and feels around for his lighter. Claudine waits for the flash of fire. Shadows wiggle in yellow light across the walls and then it is dark again. Marcus gets up and goes to the window.

"It's the circus," he says.

Claudine gets up and goes to the window to look. A guy in a sleeveless undershirt is hanging out of a boxcar. He's smoking and looking up at the stars.

Claudine lets the heat, makes the heat, relax her.

She has taken ten books of aerial photography out of the library. The walls in the front room are covered with her small paintings of the desert done in rain forest colours.

Claudine is sitting in the armchair taping together a series of photographs of the desert to make one long panoramic shot. Marcus is holding the cut up bits of leftover desert, trying to fit them into a continuous landscape.

"Claudine, you can stay here as long as you want. I mean, I don't want you to move in, but here," Marcus says, sliding open a drawer in his filing cabinet, "bring your clothes in from the car, you can have this drawer."

Marcus takes his things out of the drawer. He holds up an eight ball and a bottle of butane.

"I file things that go inside other things in this drawer."

Claudine laughs, she is sitting cross legged, her long black hair is fanned out behind her, caught in the floral texture of the upholstery. She turns her head to watch a train pass, car by car, on the other side of the road. The piercing metal howl prevents them from talking. Claudine is waiting for the last car. Just after it passes she says, "Do you remember the movies where people pressed their ears on the tracks to hear if a train was coming?"

"Claudine, if this drawer isn't enough, you can hang some of your stuff in the closet."

She turns back to Marcus and smiles.

"But listen," Marcus says, "don't start changing things around here. I like it the way it is. You sleep here practically every night anyway, you may as well bring your stuff in. I know you fit perfectly in the back of your car and all that, but I don't like you sleeping on city streets. Anyway, it's getting too cold for that. I'm going to get the gas turned back on so we'll have hot water and we'll be able to cook."

Claudine rocks forward and stands up, the cement floor is cold under her bare feet. She walks up behind Marcus and puts her arms around him. He turns around and asks, "OK?"

"Sure."

Cool light, her heart is sharp blue, waiting for clouds and rain water to fill the valley. Claudine puts black outlines around everything, heightening colours. Claudine, the green next to the black in the bass line. Black outlines all shapes, clarity where there was none.

Claudine wakes up slowly. The room is pink in the early morning. She stands up on the narrow bed with one hand flat against the adobe wall. Looking down at Marcus she bounces the bed slightly, wondering how long he'll sleep for. Claudine steps off the foot of the bed onto newspaper and splinters of wood around the fireplace. She is still looking at Marcus, thinking that his eyes appear to be sealed, not just shut. She leans closer to look at him. His eyes snap open. Claudine presses her hand against her heart.

"Morning love," Marcus says, smiling.

The waitress is pulling on Joelle's menu. Joelle is staring at her red thumb nail, she is not letting go of the menu.

"Did you want to order something else dear?"

Joelle lets go and pulls her blue wool dressing gown tighter.

The smoke from the incense stick unravels upwards. Little Christmas lights are tacked around the window. Joelle is sitting on a bench covered in purple fake fur, her legs are resting on her guitar case. She is tired. Simon and Lucky are tired. They are supposed to be quiet until the last yoga session of the day finishes in the next room, then they can start setting up for their show.

The people from the yoga studio file out, putting their coats on over skintight outfits. Their bodies are tense and angular.

D.C.

Simon is in the kitchen pricking holes in raw eggs and snipping open packages of Easter egg dye. Joelle is sitting on the front path of the house, Simon's mom's house. It is warm. The sky is a dull blue. This suburban street rises up and around a graceful corner to more egg hunts. Lily white. A man is walking down the street in sandals. He repeatedly taps his cigarette with a stiff index finger, long after the ash has dropped.

Joelle handed her dirty laundry to Simon's mom. Inside, the washing machine, the shower and the dishwasher are all going. A cat is sneaking through the yard over bits of bark and torn landscape plastic. Simon's mom is trying to keep the screen door closed to keep the mice out, she wanted to put honey on the thresholds to bring the ants out of the house, but it would have been too messy.

Simon and Lucky are standing at the picnic table in the back yard dipping hollow eggs into bowls of colour. Simon brought out plenty of his mom's heavy teaspoons to dip the eggs with, but they are using their hands. Their fingers look horribly bruised. Yellow, green, blue.

Simon is mad about the chain link fence around his mom's yard. It's new. Three kids run by on the other side of the fence. Their arms are evenly thick, like tulip stems. Busted car parts and plastic swans have been thrown over the fence. They are almost out of sight from the patio. The sun is diluted. Little rocks shine in the patio cement. Voices are smooth, smooth like mayonnaise in a glass jar. The jar slips, splitting dull on amber kitchen tiles.

Joelle whispers to herself, "In my mind my body aches."

She was the last one to find an Easter basket. She didn't want to look for it. The Easter baskets are brown soup bowls covered with plastic wrap. Three yellow bunnies lie in shredded green plastic, they are surrounded by chocolate eggs and big black jellybeans.

A smile like a turn in a wide, wide river. A smile like a snake's mouth makes a snake's eyes narrow. Mud dries on her skin on the banks of this river. Born. Don't remember, she learned to hate. Pulling hair. She tried to stab the corsage into her heart. Joelle wants a black and white photograph of the grey eyes. He could do a lot with those eyes. Offer to wash the dishes or take out the garbage. Joelle wants to paint the triangle of skin between the jeans and the sweatshirt. He is asleep.

There is a slant of gold in the grey clouds, all soft and warm over stand-up-straight-and-eat-your-peas houses on these hills. Men in white shirts have seasons for splitting wood and seasons for hunting.

In D.C. no one mentioned the grandmother. She was shuffling cards behind a curtain, she blew a whistle when she wanted something. When they were leaving, the curtain was open. Joelle saw her big face, straight grey hair and thick fingers. She was snapping cards onto a table. I Dream Of Jeannie was on the TV. The tips of Jeannie's hair shook when she talked. The sound was off.

Driving past undersea fields, Easter egg dipped trees, hot forests to walk through, cool streams to cross. Twigs in hair. Joelle walks. She walks along a cliff edge, stones roll under her feet. She is in an open field. She runs, not looking at the ground. Her breath is loud, rushing in and out. The camera lurches as she runs. She stops and settles into the grass to watch smoke signals. There are songs to sing. Love songs for love, work songs for work, dark songs at night.

Joelle is hot in her wool dressing gown. They keep driving, she sleeps for a while in the back seat. At night, in an orchard, smudged and sweaty men run full stride, pouring gas from cans. Up close their eyes reflect upside down flame. Sweat runs in fat lines down their muscled arms. Black boots press into the sticky, tractor shaped mud. The fruit trees are brittle in fire glow. Plastic lace curtains are tangled in the barbed wire fence. In the morning, the orchard will smoke in the sunshine.

OLYMPIA

The hood of Joelle's car vibrates, it doesn't close properly. She is going to live with a man she hardly knows. He told her that learning more about everything was what made him happy. Joelle liked the way he talked, his face was even and serious.

The supermarket is practically empty. They have arranged to meet here. Joelle is early. They will go to the apartment Slim has just rented. On the phone he said, "It's pretty nice."

Slim is early too. Joelle doesn't recognize him. He's got his hair slicked back and he's wearing a grey suit. They leave the store after Slim buys oven-ready biscuits, crackers, rice, white bread and cooking oil. He says, "I'll cook tonight, you can cook tomorrow night."

At the apartment Slim lets Joelle go in first. The room is grey, there is nothing on the walls. Records are spread out on the carpet. Three narrow windows face a cement wall five feet away.

"The landlord won't allow anything on the walls," Slim says. "There's something else I should tell you about the landlord, but I'll wait until after dinner."

As Joelle is doing the dishes, Slim says, "You'll have to keep a low profile, there isn't supposed to be anyone else living here."

THE DESERT, ARIZONA

Claudine grabs a rusted piece of metal and pulls it out of the bushes. Vines and branches break. It looks like a greeting card display rack. She drags it towards the back door, sets it upright and wires a broken hibachi to it at waist level. She starts to chop a leaf from the kitchen table into kindling. The hatchet blade slides easily through the length of the board. Snow flakes drift around her. She lights the fire and sets her espresso pot over the flame. With one hand in her pocket she pokes the fire to keep it going. The aluminium pot turns black, smoke blows in her face and ashes stick to her orange sweater. The coffee hisses. Steam pours out the spout, exaggerated by the cold.

Claudine pulls the cuff of her sweater over her

hand and grabs the handle. She goes up the stairs, knocking snow off her shoes. She is hoping Marcus will hear her and wake up.

The kitchen table is covered with plastic cutlery, packets of condiments and styrofoam containers. All the dishes are in the sink. Claudine finds the least rusty spoon and scours it clean. She washes two cups, pours the coffee and walks through the house to find Marcus. He is at the front window, smoking.

"Here," she says, handing him a cup.

"Thanks," Marcus says, taking the cup in both hands to warm them. He leaves the cigarette in his mouth.

"You wouldn't believe what I went through to make this."

"Claudine, I don't care if I have coffee in the morning or not. If you don't want to make it, don't."

Claudine is saturated with endings. She wonders what it will be like to never see him again.

It's 5:30 in the morning. Joelle is in a bicycle rickshaw heading for the train station. People are sleeping in the streets on flattened out cardboard boxes. Rats zigzag through them.

To get to platform five, Joelle jumps onto the tracks at platform one and goes through the trains at platforms two, three and four, jumping from train to train.

The tunnel to the sun is across the brown winter fields. Never wanting to begin, excluding appetite, holding a land candle, down in a black grit block of thought. Never yearning, never straying, muttering about a strength to ignore all tools. Bent on hesitation, anticipating the past.

Claudine wonders what it will be like never to see Marcus again.

Slim is sitting across the table from Joelle. He is listening to his Jungle Book record. He isn't saying anything about it, it's going along, loping through the scenes. Joelle isn't saying anything about it either.

In the alley a guy is spray painting his truck, he shakes the can of paint for a long time.

Slim piles macaroni onto his fork with little stabbing motions. He bites off pieces from the clump, the fork stays at mouth level while he chews.

"How do you spell meringue?" Slim asks.

"As in meringue?"

"Yeah," he says.

" M e r i n g u e, " Joelle spells, picking the hard brown bits off her pie. "I heard the check out girl at the supermarket telling someone she couldn't quit smoking because she'd have nothing else to do."

All Bays

NEW YORK

Claudine sucked the smoke deep into her lungs and held it there. She threw her head back as she exhaled, it twisted through her lips, a snake fighting the air.

Some people quit smoking when they got a cold, Claudine inhaled with more fervour.

She watched the black and white TV on the other side of the room, leaning backwards on a chair, her feet up on the back of the couch, arms crossed over her stomach. Everything in the living room was the same as it had always been. She had never liked sitting on the couch or either of the two matching chairs, she had never wanted to be part of that banal composition.

Claudine stubbed out her cigarette in the ashtray resting on her thigh. She swung her legs off the couch and jumped up, holding the ashtray at her side. She held the ashtray like an eagle holding a fish, she held the ashtray like a bowling ball. With the other hand she removed and replaced a bobby pin.

The smell of onions frying filled the room. Claudine hated the smell of onions on sunny afternoons. The onions, the couch and chairs, the black and white TV all made her uneasy. She wanted to remind herself of something else, something other than the dust in the air where the sunlight streamed through the grease streaked windows. She walked though the rooms of the house hoping that she would find other landmarks back to when she could see colour.

Claudine remembered bronze. She remembered thinking that a movie was like multi-coloured confetti in the wind. She knew that colours were symbols for other things, but she had forgotten the rules.

She blew her nose and lit another cigarette.

Daisies, peonies, poppies, irises — they were all grey. They all felt the same to her.

"Claudine, dinner will be ready in five minutes. Better wash up," her mother called from the kitchen.

"Coming," Claudine answered, grinding out a half finished cigarette in the black ashtray.

Claudine knew she hadn't always thought in black and white, dreamed in black and white. Many of her dreams were about colour, but there was no colour in them.

She pulled her black cardigan tightly around her. She only wore black and white now. If she couldn't see colour, she didn't want to represent herself with colour. She wanted some control.

Bronze. She remembered it. Strong and cold, but soft and warm at the same time. Single petals dropped in black and white, petals from different flowers. She stood still, watching them rain down around her.

"Claudine," her mother calls.

"Coming."

Claudine walks to the bathroom wondering why the TV shows are all reruns of shows she watched when she lived here as a kid. Half hour shows. There is a problem, there is a family. Someone has to make a decision between good and bad, between right and wrong. Good and right feed the family with hugs and strength. Family faces are big on the screen, big with reward. The future prevails, behavioral information is stockpiled. Proud to be proud.

Claudine looks in the bathroom mirror. Things that are black and white to other people glow. Night skies, ice fields and rivers glow. Her teeth are bright.

Claudine goes out to the kitchen, her mother is serving dinner.

"Mom, can't you please put that cigarette out? "

"Claudine, I don't understand how my cigarette can bother you when you practically chain smoke."

The smoke is biting at Claudine's throat. The

smoke and her mother's face are inseparable; bitter, pulled into grey lines and then dissipating into nothing. Her mother's solid strength wanes as the smoke sifts around the room.

Claudine thinks all sorts of things are adding up, she feels their weight, like water turning to ice, getting heavier.

Colour drips in solid language, the word rose bleeds across the sky at sunset. Claudine sees the r, the o, the s and the e spreading out thin above black mountains. A clearness she wants to call blue eyes comes to her from past dreams.

Her mother has put out the cigarette, it shines in the ashtray.

Knives and forks flash and shiver between them. Claudine remembers that the kitchen is green, a toothpaste green. The word green squeezes out of a tube, one letter at a time.

Claudine feels shaky, the air is acrid. Letters, whole words, are running by in front of her. Undulating flower petals roar down, smoke drifts up through them. Claudine can hardly see the plate on the table through the onslaught of images.

Claudine is swimming in an orange pool in the canyon where the tadpoles are bigger than the frogs. She slides down a stone chute into the next pool down the canyon. The canyon is hot.

Claudine walks up the wide, empty street. It is so bright outside. The neon sign in front of the bar is on. She pulls open the door. Black. She cannot see anything. Soon she sees Rusty's hairdo.

"Is he here?"

"No."

Outside, the street meets the horizon in a shimmer. Claudine walks towards town. It is 7 a.m.

NEW YORK

Claudine feels insulated in her studio. The walls are white, the ceiling and the pipes that run up the walls are black. The floor is grey cement. Piles of speckled river rocks are laid out around the room. Broken pieces of mirrors lean against the wall at different angles. They reflect sections of rocks, pipes and light from the tall windows. The room is smooth. Harpsichord music pours out of tiny speakers mounted near the ceiling. Waterfalls. Spoonfuls of cold water slide over pebbles. Mist resonates near the floor.

Claudine lets the sun warm her. Yellow. Her eyes are closed. Her teeth hurt. She can feel hands around her neck, she looks at the thumb print sized bruises on her arms. She can feel the pillow slamming softly into her head, a dull thud. She sways, wondering how far, how close, her head is from the wall.

"You shouldn't have gotten involved with a man who was beaten up as a kid. How many times have you been beaten up?" he sneers.

He is over six feet tall. Claudine looks at her wrists. Everything drops away, energy slides across the floor, liquid, unstuck glue. Her arms are limp, her head is pounding. The floor swims, the ceiling bubbles. He is calm, looking at a road map.

"I've felt worse than you," he says, not looking up.

The closeness is gone, his interpretations feel stale. Claudine says, "I take what I need. You hold down my hands. I take what I need and it's not you."

Claudine forces the collage of images to stop flowing. She finishes her dinner and takes the plates to the sink. She lights a cigarette and drops the smoking match into the ashtray. She walks slowly back to the living room. Her left hand cradles her right elbow, her right hand holds the cigarette to her lips. Between drags her wrist relaxes and her hand opens in front of her. She stares into her palm. Strands of hair have come loose, they fall inside the collar of her white shirt. She doesn't bother to pin them back up. Claudine smokes quickly, creating a cloud around her. The edges of the furniture soften. The sunlight illuminates the cloud. Her thoughts are crystal without distraction.

Marcus looks at Claudine. She is a small woman, but she has such power over him. He would like to be able to do anything for her, but it seems like she only wants him to do the hardest things. Claudine pinpoints weakness and shines a spotlight on it.

Swaying back and forth in the pushing and pulling of love, grinding down a belief that there is nothing worse than failure. Cold shakes through Claudine. He demands to be powerless.

Fan of sparks, flat against the sky. Falling back, not knowing there never would be new. Never would be. In the sheer blue, never having fallen before, cut to powder, it clatters like water to the floor.

Flashlights tamper with past, jittering tight around the blade. Fire swings on the mountain, weather is moving fast from the day.

Row boats are heading for the caves, they're filled with flowers. Yellow is moving slow, it ignites the grey. Watching the silhouettes of the lamplighters on the elephants in chains, they reach the wicks from the darkness, their reflections wobble on the lake.

Seven men in white shirts watch the needle on the gauge, rise and fall, swing and dive, they watch from the tower.

Claudine hears coffee percolating in the kitchen. Her mother is tuning in a radio program.

"Hi, you're on the air. Do you have a request or a dedication?"

A cheery young woman answers, "I'd like to request Girl I'm Really Going To Miss You for my baby niece who died this September eighth."

"Wow. How old was she?"

"Twenty months."

"Gee, twenty months. How did she die?"

"She got hit by a car."

The song starts, low, in the background.

"Hit by a car? How did she get hit by a car?"

"Well, she was playing in the driveway and the car started up and she was just swished into the garage door."

Claudine wonders if the call was real or not. She lights a cigarette and her smoke mingles with her mother's. She squints, licks her lips and wonders if her power dissolves as the smoke rises.

The river rocks in Claudine's room have been scattered everywhere. The mirrors have been smashed. The light bulbs that hang from the ceiling, practically to the floor, are shattered. Thin white glass juts out of the metal sockets.

Claudine clears a space on the floor, pushing the

rocks, forming new piles. The sun comes in through the tall window. She lies down in the warm rectangle on the floor. She drifts in and out of sleep, wondering what it would feel like to fall out the window. Her eyelashes make streaks on her half open eyes.

Claudine is at the window, bending out through the broken glass, staring into a blue, cloudless sky. Shards of glass sparkle on the floor and on the sidewalk below. The moon's gravitational pull has taken him, like a tide, taken those watery eyes, reacting like seas, pushing and pulling at her.

Claudine walks across the room and pulls open a sliding metal door. The fast rhythm of metal panels going over the rollers stays in her head, it lingers like an echo. The ceiling of the next room is almost entirely made up of skylights. Green safety glass tints the white walls. Claudine picks up an orange extension cord and plugs it in. For a few minutes there is a hum, then the sound of water pouring, controlled.

Claudine thinks about Marcus flying over steeples and curved river bridges in a navy blue top hat, a tux with tails flapping and a satin stripe running down the side of his pants, shining in the moonlight. Somewhere it is dark. Somewhere else. That is where Marcus is now.

Standing on the fire escape with her feet apart, Claudine alternates between focusing on the iron slats and what she can see through them in the garbage cans and cardboard boxes below. Her hair hangs down, blowing in the air that is forced to speed through the narrow alley. She steps back into the room and pushes her hair back with both hands, she digs into a bag of charcoal briquettes and piles them in the hibachi on the fire escape. She douses them with lighter fluid and tosses a match to them. Black smoke and clear flames feel around. Claudine puts a cigarette in her mouth, staring into the fire, trying to see what is between the blue centre and the surrounding heat. The striking of the match shifts her attention to the small flame at the end of her fingers. She is almost surprised to see it there.

Claudine is waiting for the coals to get hot. She is waiting for the night. The sky is changing fast, deepening to purple. The room will enclose her. The skylights will be rectangular black holes above her.

The lights on the fountain come on automatically as the room gets dark. The fountain is made up of ten plexiglas cases suspended as if they'd been tossed in the air. They are controlled, dry environments surrounded by water. An air current in one box blows sand and coloured metal flakes into piles, eroding unprotected peaks and ridges. Water flows over the cases, collecting in a pool of light. In another box there is a projected image of a fire burning ceaselessly. Water runs up, beside the flames and then spills down over them.

Claudine takes her canvas work apron off the wall and puts it on. She opens the refrigerator and pulls a frosted tray out of the freezer. She takes out the cranberry juice and drinks it straight from the jar. With her head back she looks up the wall wanting to peel away the crisp wallpaper to leave sections of each of the underlying layers exposed. She can feel the brittle paper dissolving in her hands, dry glue snapping as the thicknesses are separated, paper drifting to the floor in slow motion. Fading. Layer after layer.

The package from the freezer is thawing. Frost comes off in Claudine's hands, dripping. She can feel the hard outline of the blue-grey prawns. Rigid fins curl like sea horse tails. She scrapes off more frost and throws it onto the hot coals to hear them sizzle.

On the grill the prawns turn orange. Claudine crouches over them. Cool light, her heart is sharp blue, watching the moon, waiting for clouds and sea water to fill the alley. This air is bright light. Claudine breathes. Organdie between the black jets above the border. Sheer pink. Strong skin, pulled tight, a membrane dried in a thousand summers' eyes' frayed edges. Organdie binds the arms, an illusion of fashion. Between the hull and the sea, the boat knows how it floats. Sick of land faith, sick of gravity's mauve sheen on the alley. Believing it can't fly. Buried in hard edges, the sky's a place where planets are always round. Roads go only two ways, dying to swirl in colours without names. Roads worn by round rubber tires, softly, again and again. Planets spun smooth, pulled to a centre. Imagine the force of the void where colours don't have names.

Simon sprays on Hi Karate after shave from a gas station washroom dispenser. He gets back in the car, the smell is overpowering, but Joelle doesn't say anything. Simon talks about his uncle. He wants Joelle to agree to go to his place, out into the Superstition Mountains beyond Phoenix.

"You'll really get a kick out of this guy, he's a total sexist pig," Simon giggles and shakes his head.

Miles later, in the middle of California, Simon asks, "Didn't you notice the after shave?"

"I noticed."

"You didn't say anything, didn't you think it was funny?"

Joelle has already agreed to go to Las Vegas even though she thinks it's a bad idea. Simon has been talking about free hotel rooms and free food since Olympia.

The woman at the Las Vegas tourist booth laughs and says, "The cheapest room is $75 and you'd be lucky to find such a thing."

They walk through some casinos, free food line-ups are hours long.

"I'm an American, I believe anything," Simon says, dropping a quarter into a slot machine.

The sun is coming up by the time they find the road to his uncle's house. The uncle isn't there, but

Simon has a key.

"My uncle used to build hydrogen bombs. Pretty weird. He seems like an OK guy. That's how he ended up with the house out here. He was doing the tests in Nevada, but he didn't want to live too close to the sight."

Joelle is exhausted from the driving, but she's too jittery to sleep. She feels like crying.

Simon points to a board on the kitchen wall, it has little wooden elephant noses mounted on it.

"My uncle made this game. Want to play? You try to get these rings on the noses."

Joelle picks up a couple of the canning jar rings and tosses them limply at the noses. Her eyes blur with tears, playing a game made by a killer in the middle of nowhere.

Illusions for Film Sets

NEW YORK

Claudine is sitting on the fire escape. The moon is gone from the space between the buildings. The clouds hold its glow. Claudine measures the clouds with sections of telephone poles. She looks into the room, letting its warmth relax her. The contrast between darkness and warmth makes her feel strong. She feels the weight of all the rooms she's lived in, the cycle of replacing things. She adds the weight of all the future rooms she will live in and wonders if her power shifts as she learns her own tricks, never lessening, a river re-routed.

She gets up stiffly and goes inside, a cigarette held between her pursed lips, eyes narrow against the smoke. She picks up the box of K mart photos and slides the top one to the bottom of the pile. She is humming with the cigarette in her mouth. She is moving the photos faster, working quickly through the stack as the ash gets longer. She drops the photos back in the box and takes the cigarette out of her mouth and sings, "And you don't like strong women, they think you're a dick."

Tapping the ash off, laughing, she thinks about Marcus. She sees him in a pine forest, part of a woodcut print, sepia and black, his crumpled form lying at the base of a tree. He is chipped out of darkness, immobilized, asleep.

The sound of the freight elevator coming up changes the size and weight of the room. Joelle calls her from the other room. Claudine looks down at her white lace shirt and black velvet pants, both splattered with paint and glue.

In the other room Joelle, Simon and a man she doesn't know are unloading amps and drums from the elevator. Someone has turned on the slide projector for light, it is shining images into the elevator; paint dripping on a steel barrel, mould, sanded surfaces. Blurs of colour wrap around the three people as they bend and lift equipment. The man Claudine doesn't know is wearing white, reflecting light and colour. She figures he's the drummer. The drums are real, she can tell by the way they're being carried and set down that they're real. The metal rims scrape on the cement floor. The drums are real, the amps are real, they are not things that Joelle has made out of styrofoam, illusions for film sets.

The long light cords hanging from the ceiling are

swinging in ellipses, tracing the curves etched into the cement floor. Claudine pulls the curtain across the broken window.

"Hi you guys," Claudine says across the huge room.

"Hi Claudine."

She picks up a huge cut glass atomizer and walks towards them filling the room with a warm orange scent. An orange mist forms in front of her, a bright orange in the soft light. The atomizer is as big as a basketball.

"Mmmmmmm," the man she doesn't know says.

Claudine senses the roughness of the floor as she walks in the dark. She had wanted to polish the floor to a shine, but she ended up with a surface like dogfish skin, external teeth.

"Claudine, turn on the lights," Simon says.

She goes over to the amps and switches on a spotlight that shines up on a huge Scrabble board hanging from the ceiling on rusty chains. Steel letters are magnetically attached to it, the game is in progress. Claudine remembers the last word was hers. Ye. Marcus had objected to it and lost a turn.

"You should have called me on my first word, thermo," she had said, laughing.

"That's it. You're a cheater. Why can't you just play fair?" Marcus had said, pointing his finger at her. He was at the elevator door by the time he had finished.

"Think about it Claudine," he had called as he slide the metal gate across.

"My name's Lucky."

Lucky is standing behind her holding the kick drum, she is standing where he wants to put it down.

"Oh. I'm Claudine," she says, stepping away, moving out of the light, towards the other side of the room. She bends down and turns on a light in a small pool set into the floor. An underwater scene is illuminated. The sides of the pool are the exterior walls of an apartment building, miniature brick buildings. On the bottom of the pool there is a little patio with a swimming pool. The diving board lacks tension at four inches long. The water in the swimming pool is turquoise. Beside the pool, lying on the patio, are three dead deer. Their antlers prop up their heads at weird angles.

The speakers click on, Joelle has plugged in her guitar and the amp feeds back. Silhouettes move in front of the Scrabble board. Claudine is crouching beside the pool, she looks back into it and moves her hand slowly in the water. The scene jiggles and shimmers. The apartment buildings wobble, fluid bricks, broken lines.

"Check. Check," Joelle says into the microphone, then turns away. In a partially amplified voice Claudine hears her say, "I can hear me fine."

Joelle is in front of her amp setting the knobs. She slashes over the strings in fast sweeps and moves back to the microphone.

"Once there was the soft glow of a flare sent,
an amber fragment knocking out the sky.
Then there was the darkness after too much light,
arc fallen, wading through the snow.
Find the steel sunk below.
Fire in a half plan, shimmer up the cold.
Find the steel sunk below."

Under the guitar Claudine hears the bell for the freight elevator to be sent to the bottom. Joelle, Simon and Lucky are talking and laughing loudly.

"Claudine, we're going to play tonight. Is that OK?" Joelle asks.

"Sure," Claudine answers, closing the gate across the elevator. She sweeps up the broken light bulbs, the glass scrapes on the rough cement. Joelle is playing single notes with a lot of space around them. She adds obvious and conclusive notes, punctuation, emphasis. Her voice is low, a continuous thread in the sound.

"To the lighthouse, under jet stream.
Follow down.
Pink runs up the walls.
Paper flowers, write a letter,
say you're blue. Follow down.

Eating tears of sheep, a table cloth at dinner.
Fingers working, taking land,
spreading names on rivers.
Follow down.
Stars are warm on my back.
Come away from the wall.
Follow down."

Joelle's final guitar note is left, fading, holding onto the corners of the room, then spilling away from there as well.

Claudine takes a package of chicken livers and a can of water chestnuts out of the fridge. She fries up the livers and puts them inside pitted prunes with a water chestnut in each one. There are about thirty stuffed prunes on an oval platter. She wishes she had something else to add; kiwi fruit or golf balls or some big marbles. She looks around the room, finds six brass hinges and arranges them around the prunes.

Her eyes adjust slowly in the other room. The platter gets heavier in the dark. The orange scent seems stronger than when she left. Claudine walks between Simon and Joelle, stepping over cords and pedals. She puts the platter down on an amp and moves out of the flood of white light. From the back of the room, at the deer kill pool, Claudine hears laughter. Six women are crouched over the pool, blue reflects into their faces. Their clothes are loose, bunching up on the floor, hiding their feet. The water is moving in full waves, jagged streaks of light pulse on the walls. Claudine wonders if the deer are attached to the patio securely enough. She imagines them floating up, smacking into the apartment buildings, bobbing on the surface, rolling onto their backs with their stiff legs coming right out of the water. The deer are lustrous brown wax. Inside their heads are half ounce lead fishing sinkers with bent metal loops that the wire antlers are twisted to. Claudine thinks about gently pinching the wax to make the joints of the legs.

Marcus is waking up. His tux is wrinkled into harsh red and black lines, the blue comes back slowly as he stands up, brushing off the sepia tones of the woodcut. The pine forest softens from its motionless state, the trees become green. The wind is audible on its way towards him, it arrives in a push of the trees. Loose. Marcus is stretching, walking on the thick layer of pine needles, pressing the palms of his hands on his lower back. His knees are stiff. He turns to look at the spot where he woke up. Compositionally, he can see why this section of the landscape was chosen for the woodcut. He frames the grove of pines inside a square made with his thumbs and index fingers.

"OK, fair enough."

His clothes are damp, but the day is getting warmer. Turning away from the forest, he bends to rub his knees, his joints are really sore. An open field is spread out in front of him, it meets the sky. There is a house in the middle of the field, fences fracture away from it. Marcus can't tell how far away the house is. He closes one eye to examine perspective. The house looks more like a model of a house, a miniature example of a house or a facade. Walking towards it he looks into the sky, holding the size and weight of the house in his mind to check against when he gets closer. He does not look at the house, he keeps walking towards it.

The deer haven't come loose from the patio. Joelle is singing.

"Screen forest, sound around.
Word flywheel, how many now?
Build from where the snow fell,
season memories.
Summer stories, how many now?
We are looking at it all.
Orange light store, smooth blossoms,
cool cellar's pain.
How many now?"

Joelle's voice is a steady stream, rain hitting the ground, pin pricks in a bag of water, trailing off, sad at the end.

Burnt house, a charred skeleton, upright in the snow. The basement is like an empty swimming pool.

The camera is still following Marcus through the field. He is taking high steps through the grass, lurching towards the house. The camera is smooth, up close, then it pulls back to a vantage point in the sky. Marcus gets smaller and smaller, stumbling past the miniature house. Credits appear on the horizon, rolling up, they are in Swedish, Marcus can't read them. Bright pink letters on blue sky. Marcus falls. His breathing is loud, straight into the microphone.

The projector is mounted on a turntable. Claudine switches it on and a blur of molten colour speeds around the walls.

Beginning at the end, stepping out of it, getting smaller. Streaming out behind filaments on fire, past fouled hearts. Wading to the palace.

On the other side of the city the apartment buildings are gold. Diving deep through something more solid than water, flowers, photographs. Whole days broken into, robbing the world of hundreds of days of monotony. Surprised at the ease of being necessary. Marked. Falling back, coming up for air.

A story always only one day long, ignoring the geometry of endurance. Looking up at the surface from below, sure that it wasn't just a dream in a flash of lightning, soundless on a pink horizon. Moons roving from their courses, pulling randomly at new targets. In an instant of movement a shelter from pain is started, not evenly paced, but odd, like weather. Moving, opening up the spaces between the clouds.

Dust comes up to meet the sky, rain falls in snake shapes, finding the course of least resistance, down. Tightening everything into an absurd exclusion. Lifting heavier and heavier weights until contentment is only a memory.

Marcus' eyes are closed. His breathing is loud, the roar of breathing too close to a microphone. The roar turns into the gulping of an engine. Marcus is rolling in the field, holding onto the house. Explosions echo as it breaks into pieces. Weight, size, illusion.

Marcus is trying to reason away the cold. He is damp. The wind is steady now. He is on his back. He has lost his jacket and shirt, his purple cummerbund is sagging around his hips. His midnight blue pants are stained with yellow pollen. Marcus is thin, his ribs are waves, beautiful curves of shadow. He coughs and rolls onto his side. He is curious about the sounds around him, but he doesn't open his eyes. Speed of sound, compression waves travelling through air, steel, water. Sound waves, a million times slower than light. Claudine was always talking about light, light being pulled off its course by gravity, the weight of light. Marcus feels sad around his eyes, sad around his mouth. In the desert, yellow light echoed through everything. They watched the sun set behind the hills from the railway tracks almost every night. The smell of creosote still reminds him of sunsets.

Marcus opens his eyes and jumps up. He is on a small boat, standing unsteadily. He pushes his hands through his straight black hair. The engine is churning, the wheel is tied to keep the boat on course. Marcus steps into the wheelhouse, bending through the low doorway. He grabs the coiled cord of the shortwave radio, it snaps back loose. There is no microphone. He drops the cord and switches on the receiver. Leaning over to see the dial he turns the knob hoping to hear a transmission. The frequencies rise and fall. He tunes in a woman's voice, singing. He recognizes the song.

"I'm not in love, so don't forget it, it's just a silly phase I'm going through."

Marcus believes the woman is not in love. He thinks back to the original version, he believed the guy was in love, denying it, afraid to be in love. He is unwrapping the cellophane ends of a candy in his hands. He doesn't know where it came from. He feels like he's slipping, he's watching himself become involved in everything he encounters. The candy is on his tongue, tart and sweet at the same time. His thoughts are speeding backwards, like a thirty second sunset captured by controlled exposure film. The sun hurls itself down in a wave of fading colour, into the black. The taste in his mouth is threatening to unearth a terrible memory from childhood. He spits the candy out, it makes a hollow clunk on the wood planks. From the deck, Marcus hears a chant starting up, boys' taunting voices pour into the wheelhouse. Accusing him.

Claudine advances to the next slide, a shot of a man and a woman embracing. The woman has her arms thrown around the man's shoulders, but she is holding onto her own arms behind him. They are standing next to a Christmas tree lying beside a garbage can. Tinsel sparkles in diffused sunlight. Claudine lets the projector go through several more slides before she stops it on a shot of a salmon. The salmon swims, out of focus, around the room. Claudine sways, almost weightless in the water.

The room is crowded with people she doesn't recognize. She watches a woman at the microphone. Claudine isn't sure, but she thinks she has fishing lures dangling off her ear lobes.

The woman is talking, "I was drinking a glass of chocolate milk and reading the list of ingredients on the package. They said there were twelve vitamins and minerals in it. They've got this chart on it that lists what percentage of each vitamin and mineral you get, like your daily requirement. At the bottom of the chart it says you get eleven percent of your daily requirement of chocolate. So I wrote this haiku,

Poison drains through me
a powdered milk monologue
dissolves on my tongue."

Claudine is thinking about the house in the desert and the day she and Marcus challenged each other to a chopstick holder making contest. They went into separate corners of the yard in the bright heat and worked. Marcus bent a piece of tin into a beautiful envelope that the chopsticks fit into perfectly. Smoothly turned and trimmed metal. She made hers with a confused knot of wire and screen attached to a cement base. She built it higher and higher, trying to keep the chopsticks from tipping out.

Marcus painted the sky with her watercolours and gave her clouds, rainstorms, sunsets, stars and lightning for her birthday. The book of paintings was called Sky Villa, a Mexican bar on the south side of town. Now it seems funny to her that he would call it that. Sky Villa was a bar that he wouldn't go to in his cab, it was too dangerous to pick up a fare coming out of there.

Marcus's boat is passing between two points of land, he is listening to the engine echoing back at him across the water. He closes his eyes and imagines the sound of waves acting like light, travelling in straight lines instead of radiating out. He smiles, his face is stiff. The sound of the engine is a bright colour, the returning echo is a fainter colour, intensity lost in the distance covered.

Rollover

THE DESERT, ARIZONA

Claudine hears a car coming down the road. As it gets closer she recognizes the sound of the engine. It hits the gravel outside the house and stops. She can hear the dispatcher on the radio and the crackling, like bacon frying, between transmissions. She knows Marcus is sitting in the front seat with one leg stretched out the open door, waiting for a break so he can tell the dispatcher that he'll be out for a while.

The car door slams and he walks into the house heading for the kitchen with a foil bag of barbecued chicken.

"Claudine, dinner," he calls out.

Marcus takes plates out of the dish rack, fills a plastic jug with tap water and sits down.

"How's it going out there?" Claudine asks.

"OK," he answers unconvincingly.

He opens the bag and slides the chicken onto a plate. Licking his fingers, he pushes back his chair, ready to jump up.

"What do you need?" Claudine asks from the doorway.

"Bring a couple of glasses and a knife."

Claudine gets the Honey I Shrunk the Kids glasses and the big knife. She sits down and Marcus piles chicken on her plate. After dinner Claudine flings her bones into the backyard for the cats. Marcus takes his bones and a hammer outside for Bill, the really old cat. When they have fish it's the same. Claudine loves throwing the raw fish heads out into the dirt, watching the kittens sink their pointy little teeth in.

Marcus goes back out in the cab. Claudine picks up the knife and turns it over in her hands, imagining the force it takes to slide it between ribs. Her hands are greasy from the chicken, she holds it tighter, wondering about the resistance of skin and muscle.

She puts the knife in the sink and lazily rubs her greasy fingers on her temples.

The electricity and the gas are off. It's summer, it stays light longer, but once the sun sets it gets dark very quickly.

Claudine's thoughts are chased by dogs trapped in instamatic snapshots. The dogs eyes are red in the night. She can see into their mouths, past the teeth. She feels like she's at home in the strangest places. The sun is pounding heat, trying to get revenge. The dogs are barking, running towards her through a roll of twenty-four exposures. The dogs have questions for her.

Claudine puts her head on the train track, she hears the sea, roaring, in a straight line towards her.

The dogs have been measured out to her. Some of the snapshots have two dogs, some of the snapshots have three dogs. She doesn't know how many dogs there are, more than three, more than the ones the flashcubes illuminate.

Claudine realizes that she's looking for love in a place where smoke is dust in the sky. Marcus told her that the old woman down the street never looks at anyone. Claudine wonders why he thinks that. She is staring at a clock without hands, thinking about Marcus. She throws the clock out the front door onto the pile of junk that's been there as long as she's known him. He threw all his last girlfriend's stuff out there. She looks down at the underwear and the black leather skirt with the piece cut out that Marcus used to patch his jeans.

Lightning flashes silently behind the hills, buoyancy in the darkness. Solidity pulsates. This light works on her. Police helicopters shine down spotlights. It starts to rain. She gets in her car and drives towards the hills, towards the desert, to hear the thunder. She stops and rolls down the window. Rain pours in, she puts her bare arm out and watches the water run off. The sky is filled with more electricity and light than darkness. The thunder is everywhere, a constant roar.

Claudine gets out of the car and a river of water and stones moves around her feet. She jumps over a ditch and figures out where the cactus are in the flashes. Water is running down her neck and dripping off the ends of her hair. She's climbing a hill, stones move under her feet, loosened by water. Slipping forward, her hands sink into gravel and wet earth. She looks behind her to see how far she's come, pulling at hair plastered across her face. The desert curves below. She staggers, unbalanced by the rain in her eyes. Facing the hill again, she tries to run. The thunder is like steel doors slamming behind her.

Making it anything so it isn't nothing now, touching at the future with a tin edge hollow stamp. Weaving the spin of endurance, knots hanging in black twine, jarred up on a plank shelf, oiled to a dull shine. Wanting, wishing, for wind to knock this stillness out. This machine rides. Pounding up loud, sifting freight tight on a sigh.

Claudine is soaked, she cinches her belt up one notch, her jeans are weighed down with water.

Crystals splinter and hiss against the sky. The valley is filling up with water. The boatmen are standing on the shore, motionlessly waiting for the right moment to cast off in the storm. They are holding their oars straight up, waiting for the water to rise.

Water runs in veins down the varnished wood.

In town, the storm is already over. Everyone is calm and dry, walking slowly under street lamps. The lightning is still flashing in the hills. Claudine breathes deeply. The desert is on thin time. There is no anticipation in the air. Reaction is a long steel shaft carefully filed to a point. Reaction is the weapon of choice. Anger is the visible heat collecting in the dips on the highway.

Claudine's eyes are closed. She opens them and they feel like magnets, pulling to her what she doesn't want. She is sitting at the bar in the Hotel Congress, chewing grape gum and drinking glass after glass of beer. Joelle says, "I remember the cowboy curtains from when I was a kid in here. I was five years old and my dad bought me Shirley Temples all day while he got plastered on gin and tonics, an endless number of gin and tonics. I remember thinking that he must really like these drinks."

Claudine dumps some M & Ms into Joelle's open hand. Joelle gives back the colours she doesn't want. She swears she didn't put I'll Fall To Pieces on twice in a row on the jukebox.

The smell of diesel is giving Marcus a headache. The water is getting rough. A bottle of booze starts to roll around over the wooden planks. Marcus watches the dark liquid forming little waves inside the bottle. He closes his eyes.

Claudine watches the willow tree blowing, slow, like seaweed, breaking up the consistency of the street light.

"Where's Marcus tonight?" Joelle asks.

"He's driving," Claudine answers.

"He seems to be working all the time now."

"Twelve hour shifts almost every night, then he sleeps all day. He's not even making any money at it though. The electricity is off again, there's not much point in hanging around there in the dark."

Joelle is helping a blind guy next to her to organize the bills in his wallet in sequence. The bartender looks like he thinks she'll rob the guy. The TV is flashing, the sound is off. The blind guy says, "I'm the best cane traveller in the state of Arizona."

He is facing straight ahead, Claudine watches him in the mirror behind the bar. The bartender is leaning against a rack of bottles looking at his fingernails. The blind guy continues, "I'm smart and there's nothing they can do about it. I've got an I.Q. of 167 and I love knives, I can make knives sing, but my passion is for automatic weapons. They won't let me have any because I'm blind. I tell you, I'd shoot anyone who tried to burn the flag."

He slams down his empty glass and yells for another beer. The bartender is right in front of him.

Joelle spins around on her stool, walks over to the jukebox and starts reading out the song titles. The blind guy doesn't realize she's gone, he keeps talking, "I'd love to be employed by the C.I.A. This country is the best the world has to offer. I would do whatever was necessary to stop the enemy."

Marcus is on his back. He is holding a tiny egg at arm's length. He closes one eye to measure the roundness of the egg against the bright blue of the sky. The old window glass ripples the brilliant light. Marcus's fingers are cold. He is thinking about the little bird in the egg. His hands are shaking badly. The egg breaks. Marcus holds the sticky lump of shell and bird in both hands on his chest. He breathes deeply, his chest rises, his hands stop shaking for a few minutes.

The sun works over his body. The sun is a squared off shape moving across the room, it bends up and over him. His head is filled with underwater colours, he wants to clear the swimming blur. He rolls over on his side and rakes his fingers through his hair, pulling at the tangles.

Outside, the fluid sensation turns to forest. Branches snap, leaves brush against his face. The pinwheels of light don't distract him from going farther into the forest. He stops when he can't push his way any deeper. The only sound left is the river. Marcus looks back at the house and the rusted truck half sunk in the river bank sand.

Marcus hears the new pick-up before he sees it,

flashing red between the trees, bouncing in and out of mud puddles. His eyes ache remembering the strain of watching clouds in puddles.

The truck door slams, a woman walks heavily to the house carrying a bag of groceries and a case of beer. Marcus listens to her boots on the wooden stairs. She stops on the porch and looks around. Her voice is clear and strong above the river.

"If you can hear me give me a sign. I'm still waiting for advice. I don't know whose angel you are, but I need your help again."

She puts the beer down to open the door. Inside, the bag collapses and packages of instant noodles spill out.

"Damn. Roy Henry!" she yells.

Marcus starts to call out in reply, but he stops himself, slapping a hand over his mouth. A crow circles above him, screeching down at him. Marcus rubs his sticky, gritty fingers together. He walks to the truck sunk in the sand and climbs in the back. He picks up a half burned stick and runs its charcoal end across the rusty metal. The noise, the soft jagged noise is enough. He lies down. From the house he hears glass shattering.

"Roy Henry!"

The voice is diluted in his head by the thickness of the charcoal on the rough metal. Oceanic roar. The blue sky is fading to a haze. Marcus thinks about the little eyelashes on the dead baby bird. His fingers sift the ashes and bits of charred wood that cover the back of the truck.

Joelle and Claudine walk over to the Greyhound station, to the photo booth. They want photos of each other before Claudine goes back to New York. Everyone says how much they look alike. The pictures turn out like mug shots; one profile, two straight ahead, none of them smiling.

They walk down 4th to Joelle's apartment, waving wet photos in the hot night air. Joelle wants to play a tape of her singing for Claudine. The apartment has a very high ceiling, through the skylight a palm tree flickers in the moonlight, one of the tallest and oldest palm trees in town. Joelle has mannequin parts all over the place. Claudine tries to put the bodies back together in her mind. Joelle stops and starts the tape, trying to find the part she wants to play.

"I recorded it riding my bike around in the swimming pool when it was empty."

The music starts and Joelle sings.

"Bicycle handlebars scrape across the suburbs.
Chrome to iron, innocence chips off.
There are desperate, harsh attempts
at simplicity
by people who know too much.
The soft white wax of a candle

goes hard
when the flame is blown out.
You are taking the backstairs."

The bike is propped up amongst the torsos. There are streamers on the handle bars and woven into the spokes. There is a wicker basket wired to the front with plastic flowers all over it. Joelle is putting their photos in with the flowers.

Joelle and Claudine put on roller skates and head back downtown, laughing and singing. Marcus is parked at the Greyhound, Claudine skates over to the car.

"If you didn't have those skates on you could come out with me for a while."

"Marcus, I'm going back to New York. You can come if you want. This is crazy sitting around down here."

"I'm not wild about this either, but I've got to make some money before I can go anywhere. I figure after New Year's Eve I'll have enough."

"New Year's Eve? Marcus, it's August, what are you talking about?"

Joelle is buying a tube of Indian eye-liner from a woman in a tent at the market.

"Why do you want this? It's old fashioned. All the girls are wearing eye-liner from London."

Joelle walks through the hot courtyard of her hotel and opens the turquoise shutters to her room. She steps into the darkness. She turns around and sees the boy who sells tea standing in the doorway, a silhouette. He is balancing the wire tea basket on his hip. A man wearing sunglasses steps into the doorway, takes two glasses of tea and comes into the room. He puts the tea on the low table and sits down. He takes off the sunglasses and slides them into the pocket of his polyester jacket.

"Do you like the room? Is everything OK? Can I do anything to make your stay more comfortable?"

Joelle has moved to the door. The boy is still standing there.

"Everything is fine."

"How about if I pick you up tomorrow and we go for a ride in my car? I'll show you the sights. You should have proper clothes though. We'll stop by my tailor's and have an outfit made for you. We can pick it up in the evening and then I'll take you out for dinner. What time should I come and get you?"

"I don't think this is a good idea."

He is waving his finger at her saying, "No, no. Just say what time."

Joelle asks, "Do you own this place?"

"No, no. I saw you come in here from the street. I wanted to talk to you. What time should I pick you up tomorrow?"

"Look, I want you to leave," Joelle says to the man.

"I'll drop by in the morning to see if you've changed your mind."

He puts the sunglasses back on and walks out. Joelle looks in the mirror, the eye-liner has melted and smudged all around her eyes.

Rebar

THE DESERT, ARIZONA

Claudine is sitting at the darkest booth in the restaurant. The seats are slashed up red vinyl. A man and a woman are sitting at a window table, the red bounces up, lighting his face from below. Claudine can't see the woman's face, but she watches as her glowing red hand lifts forkfuls of food. The man is leaning forward.

"Do you understand me?"

"I don't know why you don't want to build it flat. Why do you need to dig?" she asks.

"It's like a cake. You know when you're baking a cake? Are you following this?"

"Why do you have to dig?"

"It's the foundation. Christ. You put in the rebar, pour the cement, use boards for the form. You ever baked a cake?"

"Yes I baked a cake, but I don't want to live underground."

"Right, we're going to dig down and make a cave and we're going to live in it, in the dirt."

"I'm not digging," she says, folding her arms over her chest.

"I need help, you're going to help me, you can lift a pick."

"I can't."

The man crumples his napkin and drops it on the shredded lettuce on his plate. He looks out the window into the glare.

Claudine is chipping glue off her fingernails. She looks at the test tubes in the wooden stand and starts to drop purple beads into the heavy oil, trying to pace them evenly, making them sink like the June Taylor Dancers kicking in kaleidoscopic patterns. Some of the beads stick to her fingers, others spill and roll away inaudibly. She pours mixed geometric glitter shapes down the crease of a plastic bag, sprinkling stars, circles and triangles into the oil. They float for a moment before falling slowly, collecting in the round end of the tube.

Marcus opens his eyes. He is curled up in the back seat of a car. Foam rubber is coming out of the frayed upholstery. The car windows have drops of water on them, they reflect the colour of the sky, white. Marcus sits up stiffly and looks at a wood fence beside the car. The water drops make it look like it has hundreds of knotholes in it. Three starlings are sitting on the fence. Marcus closes one eye to make sure there are really three, something about the window and the reflections make him feel like the bird image is being multiplied. With one eye closed there are still three birds.

The car is parked on a hill, at the bottom of the hill there is a frozen lake. A half submerged house is frozen into the middle of the lake at an angle, tipped.

The chimney points at him like a tank cannon.

Marcus opens the car door and gets out onto the gravel road. He exhales a cloud of steam and slams the door, it echoes in the hills. The camera lens blurs the edges of the lodge pole pines every time Marcus exhales. The camera pans to the house in the ice. Marcus exhales and the house practically disappears in diffused white light. Soaked into a cloud of vapour.

Marcus hears a car coming along the gravel road. A truck with a camper on it appears. The guy driving is wearing a hunting cap and a bright orange jacket. He pins his eyes on Marcus, watching him without moving his head. Silver writing on the bevelled side of the camper stay in Marcus's mind. Fun-seeker. Marcus weighs the set of letters in his hands, round cold letters, shiny on the front. The other side is dull metal with pegs that push through the camper. The blue eyes of the hunter are big in front of him. He turns the letters over and over in his hands. The hunter's heavy rimmed glasses are held together at the hinges with band aids. Flares of blue shoot out from the pupils, so blue they look purple. The rifle in the gun rack appears to run straight through his head, like an arrow.

The camera finds the place where the truck first came into view, it follows the truck's route, moving faster towards the point where it passed Marcus. The camera focuses on the road where the truck disappeared around a curve. Water drops have fallen on the lens, light spirals, fracturing into rainbows.

Marcus searches his pockets for car keys, he looks in the car, checking the ignition. No keys. He looks around his feet, strips of movie film are blowing across the gravel.

Smoke is coming out of the chimney of the house. A window is opening upwards, like a hatch cover on a boat. A bottle of booze comes flying out the window. A pair of snowshoes follow, one at a time. The house, the bottle and the snowshoes have turned into a drawing, a cartoon. The smoke is coming out of the chimney in a pencil wisp. A gong crashes and an iron frying pan sails out the window. The front door swings open and a cartoon cat jumps out and staggers around on the ice to the sound of a slide whistle. The cat's face has been flattened in, it shakes its head in a scribble of pencil marks and its face pops back to normal. A bloated yellow bird floats out the window blinking its wide eyes. The bird had long eyelashes.

Marcus starts to feel sick, warm tears are running down his cheeks. A shot is fired, Marcus ducks and leans against the car. The shot has a funny tone, it doesn't echo. The music continues, another dull shot is fired and the bird is replaced by a confusion of yellow feathers. A second later the bird reappears.

A cartoon man with a mustache and a ten gallon

hat sticks his head out the window. He levels the gun at the bird, but before he can fire, the house starts to slide farther into the lake. The man falls into the house with a series of thumping sounds. The house goes under as the slide whistle descends.

The cat's legs are windmilling above the ice, his fat paws reach out for the bird. The cat takes off leaving little clouds of smoke at his heels. They both disappear weaving through the trees beyond the lake.

Marcus is crying, he is cold. A song is running through his head.

"Collapsed cardboard box house,
knife slice for windows.
It's dark inside. Hollow.
You can't fool yourself,
you know all your tricks.
A lump of coal in your temple,
I huddle near it like it's fire.
She's hurt and wondering why,
he hurt her, she's wondering why.
Too close to the fire
in the cardboard box house
of love."

There is a rustling sound all around Claudine. Her eyes are closed. She stretches out her hands, pushing her arms through folds of slick fabric. She is wrapped tightly. She hears a cello, the music is low, densely muffled.

Claudine opens her eyes, all around her is smoothness. Pink, violet, purple, crimson silk twist her body's length. She brings her hands to her face and unravels lavender. There is fabric above her, she moves up through it, kicking like a swimmer surfacing. She bends to free her legs from rose and purple, silk creasing, cool between her legs. The cello bow never stops on the strings.

Claudine's splayed fingers move down her legs, the silk roars in her ears. She closes her eyes, immersed in resistance. The warm wood of the cello, bent into curves, hollow, breathing in time. She dives down, slow motion struggling, trapped in folds of weighted colour. The silk tints her skin, pinks and purples melt over her, shadows make her round. Her heart is pounding, she can't place herself in this depth.

Darkness changes the colours to tones of grey. Claudine pulls her knees to her chest. The cello stops. She dreams of turning over river rocks, looking into the rounded out shapes left in the mud. Water runs like music all night. In her dream she plans a circle. Drawn on paper, it is folded, an oval in her pocket. She is approaching Marcus, his back is to the river, high above it, on a cliff. He falls. He falls, an arch, into the river. His eyes following a bigger arch in the sky. The land tilted. He leaves a copper pipe outline where he stood. Hot water gone cold around his form. The copper shines in the sun.

Claudine wakes up as the cello is being tuned. She finds the bottom, it is as rough as sandpaper. The silk is frayed into dull strands and tendrils. On her hands and knees she moves across the bottom looking for the sides. The heap of silk above her is weightless, it crushes in on itself. The cello is everywhere, clear and sharp, a tongue sliding across teeth, taunting her.

She finds the side, knocking on it to test its strength. She stands up and kicks, a panel falls into the darkness of the other side. She crawls through and stands up. Lights come up theatrically. A gold spotlight illuminates a ladder, burnt to charcoal, but still intact, leaning against a wall. The top of the ladder extends beyond the light. Another soft spotlight is on the cello and the arms of the cellist. The bow is held, motionless, above the strings.

Claudine walks through the dark space between the ladder and the cello. Gradually, a light made up of all colours fills the sky. The memory of the cello is replaced by the sound of flowers opening and clouds building up. Roundness has a big sound. Increasing brightness pushes the volume higher. Claudine is at the edge of a black lake watching white light ripple its surface. She rests her eyes between the pressure of sound, light and water. Wind enlivens the white splintering across the lake, it sharpens sound to a siren pitch. In one continuous movement Claudine leaves the shore and submerges.

The blackness holds heat. The lake is so warm. Claudine glides underwater, thin reeds touch her like long slippery fingers. Farther out, fish swim to her and turn against her body. When she comes up for air, the wind is fresh in her face. The smell of flowers is so strong, travelling across the flat lake at twice the speed of sound. The lake is a fine conductor for scent. She sinks back into the water so that her eyes are level with the surface. Waves lap up and blur everything to soft grey.

Claudine goes under for longer and longer periods of time. Her eyes adjust to the light below. She becomes more relaxed with the pushing and pulling of water. Claudine dives down deeper, she doesn't need much air to sustain her. She hums a song that weaves bubbles in front of her and past her ears. The melody descends, low notes are held a long time. Claudine pivots, a pirouette, an axle in space. The bubbles twist around her body, spheres of light and sound.

"I row my boat to shore.
I pull up on the sandy beach of spite.
I walk across the sand
to the dark, to the trees.
I look back over my shoulder,
the sea sucked my boat away.
The sea grows cold, the sky, grey.
It pounds down rain.
No escape. I've been here for twenty years
in the sea line, grey line, cloud line.
Twenty years, no escape."

Claudine knows Marcus's last letter by heart.

"It's too bad we couldn't have met as simpler animals in another time. We are both too fucked up to keep doing this. I am playing out a scenario that has existed in me for all time. You are using me to get revenge on your past. No wonder I dream of islands."

INDEX

MECCA NORMAL
is available on LP, CD and cassette

Mecca Normal (1986) Smarten Up! Records
re-released (1993) K Records

Calico Kills The Cat (1988) K Records

Water Cuts My hands (1991) Matador

Dovetail (1992) K Records

Jarred Up (1993) K Records

Flood Plain (1993) K Records

JEAN SMITH
7" record

Carboni Angel (1992) Kill Rock Stars
a spoken word excerpt from
I Can Hear Me Fine

K Records
p.o. box 7154
Olympia, WA 98507
U.S.A.

K Records are distributed by Cargo